# Hooray for Oklahoma

# 1889

B.C. Publishing

Broken Arrow, Oklahoma

Hooray for Oklahoma, 1889
Copyright 1989 by B.C. Publishing
Text copyright 1989 by Carolyn Kirschstein
Illustrations copyright 1989 by David Merrell

Printed in the United States of America.

First Edition

To order additional copies contact:

B.C. Publishing
P.O. Box 2102
Broken Arrow, OK 74013
(918) 357-3285

Library of Congress Catalog Number: 89-060208
ISBN 0-926521-00-4

# Contents

To all the '89ers who were brave
enough to tame this territory for
future generations of Oklahomans
and to Sarah Ashley — one of those
future generations.

**1** Red People's Land
*Page 5*

**2** Dreams
*Page 11*

**3** Plans
*Page 15*

**4** April 22, 1889
*Page 23*

**5** The Rush
*Page 33*

# Chapter 1

# Red People's Land

Joey and Jane could hardly wait for tomorrow. It was the biggest thing that had ever happened in their young lives. Pa was happier than they had ever seen him. He was also worried.

Joey walked around Smokey, his shiny black pony, and checked all the riggings. It wouldn't do to have the cinch on his saddle break, not tomorrow. Tomorrow was too important. Pa was checking his saddle, too. He also looked at the map one more time. He felt for the wooden stakes in his saddle bags with the name Taylor written on each one. Then he turned back to his red and white pinto and walked around feeling the horse's ankles and knees. He wanted no problems. Not tomorrow.

Jane wanted to go, too. It wasn't fair. She could ride just as well as Joey, but Pa said it was too dangerous. And Joey was going only because Pa had promised. "I guess Pa's right," thought Jane, "someone needs to stay with Ma and baby Lisa, but it's so important and I want to go."

Jane's thoughts went back to the rainy spring day that Pa had returned home from town all excited. In his hand was a paper with lots of words, but Jane saw only the two words in big, black, bold letters — LAND RUN. Further down the page she read in smaller letters—Oklahoma Territory.

8

"What is Oklahoma Territory," asked Jane, "and how can land run?"

Pa had laughed. "If we travel west, young lady, we'll be in Red People's land, Okla(people) and homa(red). It's called a territory because it's not a state like Missouri. We won't go to watch land running. We'll go to join the run for the land. This notice says the United States Government wants people to settle in Oklahoma Territory. The government will give away 160 acres of land to anyone who will live on it and farm it. But we can't just go and pick it out."

About that time Joey became interested in Pa's piece of paper. "How do you get it, then?" asked Joey.

"As near as I can figure, everyone lines up at noon on April 22 and runs to stake a claim on a piece of ground he wants to farm. But you have to be the first one there, so it's kind of like a race." answered Pa.

"How fast can we run in our boots, Pa?" asked Joey. There went Pa's laugh again. "It would be faster if we rode a horse, Joey."

# Chapter 2

# Dreams

Ma and Pa talked long into the night. Jane and Joey heard part of their talk before falling asleep. Jane began to realize how much it meant to Pa to own their own farm. He was tired of farming someone else's piece of ground. Ma wanted Pa's dreams to come true, but she knew how hard it could be to make a living off the land. This Oklahoma was surrounded by Indian Territory.

"What kind of Indians?" she asked Pa. "Are they friendly?"

"All I know is that the Indians have their own assigned lands — land where they farm and live and hunt. This land rush is in an area that wasn't assigned to any Indian tribe and its our chance to farm our own piece of ground. I've just got to try, Ma. I've just got to." said Pa.

So it was that Pa and Joey began to make their plans.

# Chapter 3

# Plans

The Taylors owned 5 horses, all were plow horses. They were big, tough and strong for pulling a plow through the dirt and pulling a wagon loaded with supplies to and from town. Two of those horses pulled Jane, Joey and Lisa and Ma and Pa to church every Sunday in the Buckboard wagon. They were strong, but they were not fast. Fast horses were what Pa and Joey needed.

Pa took his 3 best plow horses to town
where he traded them for 2 quarter horses.
He had found a black pony named Smokey
and a red and white Pinto called Big Red. The
horse trader had been generous and had
included 2 saddles with the trade. It was risky
trading his best plow horses for a chance at
160 acres of land but Pa knew he had to try.

Smokey was just the right size for Joey
and since Joey was not nearly as heavy as Pa,
Smokey should be able to run as fast as Big
Red. Joey thought Smokey was wonderful
and practiced riding him every day. Soon, it
looked like Joey had been riding a horse all
his life. Jane was not to be outdone by her
older brother. She, too, wanted her turn on
Smokey every day. If Smokey were to choose
the better rider, Jane would be his choice.

While Joey was becoming accustomed to Smokey, Pa was taking care of other important matters. He needed to know:

1. Where to start the run
2. How far to the unassigned lands
3. How to stake and register the claim
4. How to get there first.

By talking to others interested in the Land Rush and to government agents, Pa's plans slowly began to take form. He and Joey would be ready on April 22, as ready as any man and boy could possibly be.

Another kind of plan was beginning to form in Jane's thoughts. Maybe, just maybe, on this 160 acres there would be a place Jane could have for her very own.

"What do you want with some land of your own?" Pa had asked.

"Not a very big place," Jane had answered, "I want to plant a garden. Not a vegetable garden — I know we'll have to have one of those. I want a garden just to look at — just a small one for flowers."

"Now little lady, just what kind of flowers do you propose to grow?" Pa had teased.

Jane had teased back, "I'll grow ones with all the colors of the rainbow, but especially roses like the ones in front of the BIG houses in St. Louis."

So Pa had his dream and Jane had hers. Now on this Easter Sunday they were getting ready for their dreams to come true. Easter is a time of hope and new beginnings. Maybe tomorrow would bring a new beginning for the Taylor family.

# Chapter 4

# April 22, 1889

At sunrise on Monday, the 22nd of April, 1889, Pa and Joey emerged from their tent on the Northern border of Oklahoma Territory. They spent the morning helping Ma and Jane with breakfast over the campfire. Then they fed and watered Smokey and Big Red. Joey carefully brushed his black pony and walked him around the camp to warm up the muscles in his legs.

When the sun was directly above them, Pa and Joey saddled their horses. Following the rules of the land rush, Pa and Joey lined up on the border behind the army troops who were to signal the start of the run.

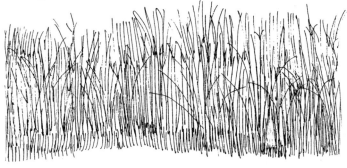

Joey looked around him and saw the men
on horseback. Some were big, rough, tobacco
chewing men. Some were men with strong
arms and strong hands who plowed the land.
These were the farmers like his Pa. There

26

were even a few women dressed for a long ride. Some rode horses and some traveled in wagons. There were hundreds of horse riders, wagon drivers and walkers. If they could make it, Joey knew he could make it, too.

"Is it almost noon yet, Pa?" asked Joey. "I don't think it's ever going to get here. I'm ready to ride — right now."

"You don't want to be one of those Sooners the Federal agents hauled back to the border yesterday, Joey. The rules say no one enters Oklahoma Territory before noon today." said Pa.

Joey settled down and waited for the sound of the pistols and bugle call to signify the opening of the lands. He hoped nothing would happen — no accident, no lame horse, nothing. With all these people, anything might happen.

"I'm worried, Pa." said Joey. "There are so many horses and riders I might lose you."

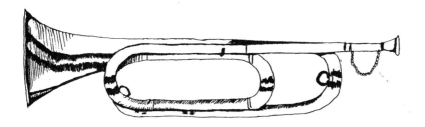

"Stay close," answered Pa, "you can always see Big Red. When the bugle sounds, ride with all your might. I know where I'm going even though I've never seen it. The maps have told me how to get there and it's all memorized in my head.

As the hands of Pa's pocketwatch approached 12 o'clock noon, Joey turned around and saw a sight he was to see only once in his life.

Many people had decided to ride the train
from Arkansas City to the unassigned lands.
They had already been traveling for more
than two hours to reach the border by
noontime. Passengers hung out of windows
waving flags and cheering "Hooray for

Oklahoma." Some had even hitched a ride on the top of the cars. It was like a holiday and no one wanted to be late. Some had been afraid the heavily loaded train would not make the border on time.

"Look Pa," yelled Joey. "More people are coming. Can we beat the train?"

"It's one minute 'til noon — Big Red and I are ready. How about you and Smokey?" asked Pa.

Joey answered, "We've been ready since sunrise, Pa."

"Then we'll make it," Pa quietly replied.

# Chapter 5

# The Rush

Finally, both hands on Pa's pocketwatch pointed straight up. Pa and Joey held tight to their horses' reins and pushed a little closer to the line of army troops. Suddenly the bugle sounded the "Dinner Call" and the troops rolled back to let the galloping, yelling, hopeful horsemen over the border.

The thickness of the dust almost caused Joey to lose sight of Big Red. But Pa had been right — Big Red was always there. They rode in the middle of the group for what seemed like forever. At the top of a hill, Pa suddenly turned to the west and Joey had a chance to look back. He saw the wagons far behind them and watched the train continue straight south. It was traveling to the townsite of Guthrie. Pa and Joey were headed toward the 160 acres Pa had picked out near the Cimarron River.

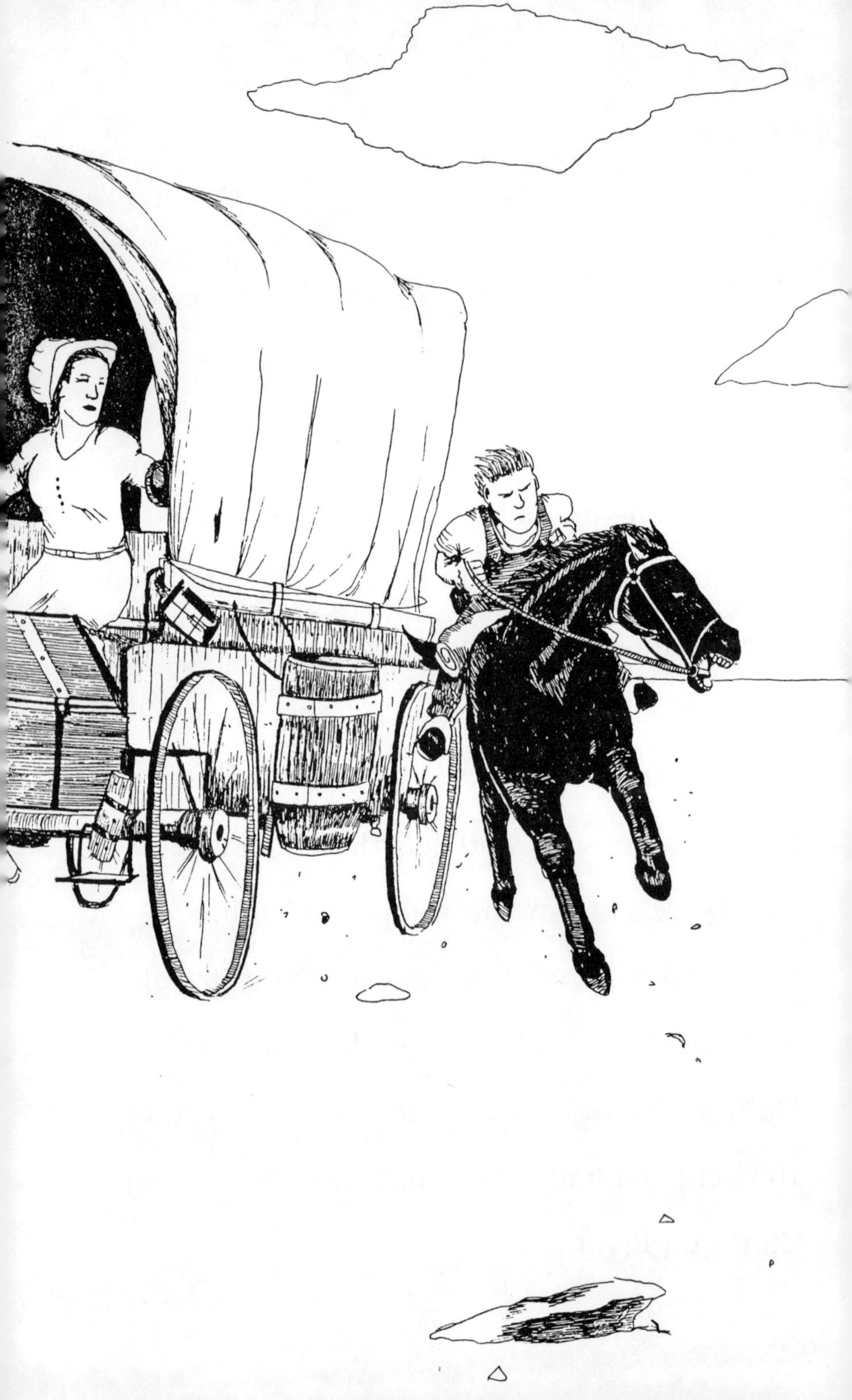

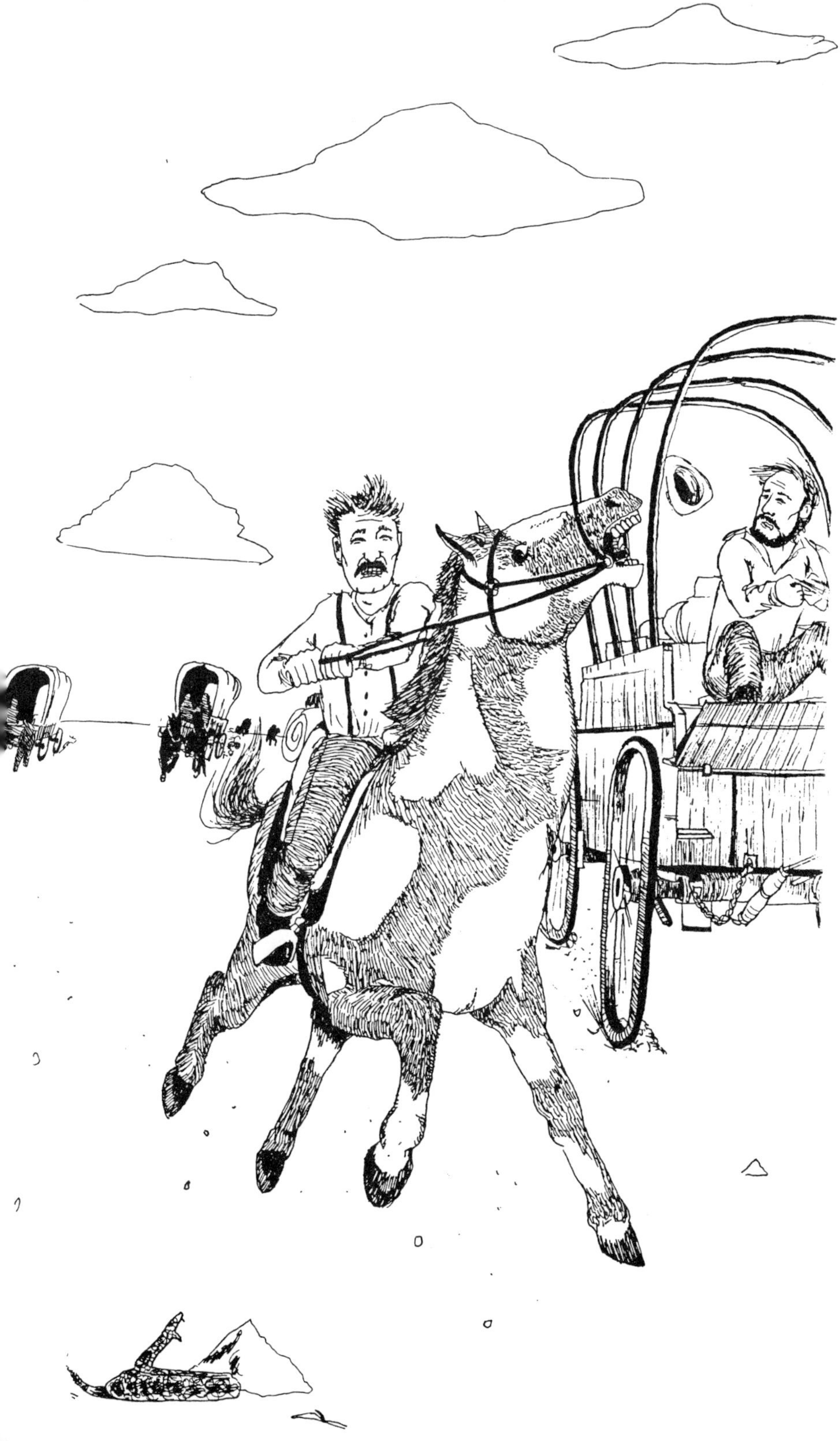

Using the map memorized in his head, Pa directed Big Red across the prairie. Joey and Smokey were not far behind. They passed the white tents of those who were happy to claim land nearer the border.

The two of them rode long and hard. It was dusty and hot and the horses were beginning to tire. Pa yelled, "It's not much farther, Joey." Joey breathed a sigh of relief. But then his worries returned, "What if someone else had staked a claim on Pa's land? They had sold their plow horses and most of their furniture for the chance at a farm of their own."

Over the next ridge, Joey could see a river in the distance. Suddenly Pa yelled, "We're here." And he began to dismount. He quickly grabbed the four stakes from his saddlebag — the ones marked with the name Taylor. Pa started driving one of them in the ground. Joey took another and rode to the next corner of the 160 acres and drove it into the ground. When all four stakes had been driven, Pa and Joey had another job to do.

The claim had to be registered with the land office at the townsites of Guthrie or Kingfisher. While Joey set about making a shelter from the sun and heat, Pa rode to the nearest land office at Kingfisher. He would show the agents just where his claim was located on the map. The agents would then give him a deed telling everybody that the land belonged to James Joseph Taylor.

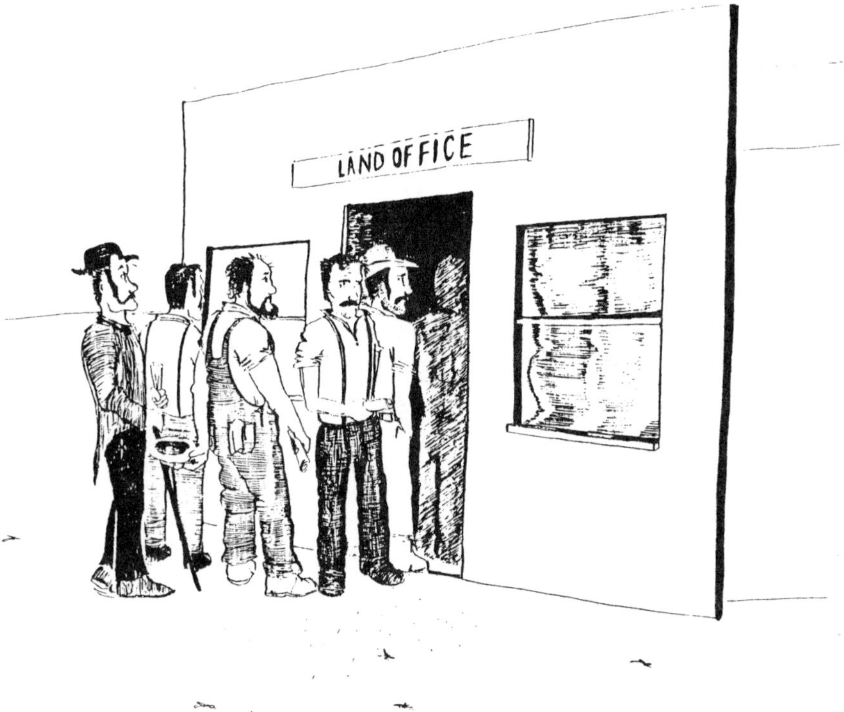
LAND OFFICE

As the sun slowly moved toward the
western sky, Joey fell asleep in his shelter
made from the branches of trees and brush.

He had removed his bedroll and saddle
from Smokey so that the tired pony could rest
from the hot and dusty ride. Others on
horseback passed by him. They did not
bother him or try to claim the land as their
own. As Joey would later find out, there were
many disputes over some of the claims. Joey
and Pa were lucky that day.

Joey awoke to the sound of Pa's excited yells, "We did it, Joey, we did it. The land is ours."

Surprised to see that it was already dark, Joey yelled back, "Hooray for Oklahoma."

"I had to stand in line at the land office for six hours to register our claim. There were so many people behind me in line that some of them will be waiting for days." said Pa. "We'll show our land to Ma and Jane and Lisa tomorrow."

Both of them slept well the rest of the night.

# Chapter 6

# Roses

On Thursday, the Taylor Family awoke in
their tent on their own farm. They had spent
two days getting the horses and wagon with
all their belongings from the border.

All Jane could think about was where she would plant her garden of rainbows and roses. It would be fun to explore the 160 acres of prairie and grasslands that were to be their home forever.

"It's my turn to ride Smokey," announced Jane as she saddled the black pony. "You got here first," she told Joey, "but I get to explore it first.

"Wait a minute, little lady," exclaimed Pa, "you can't just go trotting off by yourself. Didn't you ever hear of rattlesnakes?"

"Come with me, Pa. I can't wait a minute longer or I'll just bust," said Jane.

"To tell you the truth, I can't wait either," said Pa, "Let's go." And he mounted Big Red.

As they rode, Pa explained there were lots of things to do. Trees must be cut. Fields must be plowed and planted. A small cabin needed to be built until there was time to build a larger house. They must find a spot to grow a vegetable garden so there would be food for the summer and winter. The horses, the milk cow and the chickens needed a shelter.

You forgot something," said Jane. "You forgot my garden just to look at. Where can I plant the roses?"

"Just keep looking around," said Pa, "I know you'll find exactly the right spot."

"Look at those big trees," said Jane.

"There are three of them and their leaves are

green like Springtime. Let's go sit in the

shade for awhile."

As they dismounted, Jane spotted some reddish-looking rocks not far from the three Cottonwood trees. The rocks were sitting in a cluster, just as if someone had carefully placed them inside an imaginary circle.

Jane bent down and picked up the largest of the sandy red rocks. Turning it over, she noticed that it was different from any other rock she had ever seen. She replaced it in the circle and picked up a smaller one. Surprisingly, it looked a lot like the larger red rock. Carefully, she examined each of the rocks with growing excitement and wonder.

She took the rock she liked best and put it in her pocket to show Pa.

"I don't have to look any further for my garden spot," she said to Pa. "In fact, I don't even have to plant a garden. Someone already planted it for me."

"You're teasing me, again," replied Pa. "The only red things I see around here are the rocks."

Jane reached in her pocket and held out the pinkish-red sandstone for Pa to see.

"See," said Jane, "it looks just like a rose and there's a whole garden of them right where we can build our house."

Pa and Jane gave each other a big hug.

"Hooray for Oklahoma," yelled Jane. Then she and Pa raced back to tell Ma and Joey and Baby Lisa.

# Understanding
# Oklahoma

**Boomers** — a group of people that asked the U.S. Government to open the public lands in Oklahoma Territory for homesteading. They wanted to go "booming" into the new lands and organize the creation of a new state.

**Sooners** — persons who entered the unassigned lands before noon on April 22, 1889, in order to claim their land before anyone else. It was against the rules of the Land Run to do this.

**Guthrie** — Capital of Oklahoma until 1910.

**Unassigned Lands**—Public lands. Lands not assigned to any Indian tribe. Much of Oklahoma Territory had been assigned to Indian tribes such as the Choctaws, Chickasaws, Cherokees, or Creeks.

**Oklahoma** — became a state in 1907. Charles N. Haskell was the first governor of the new state.

**Roserock** — a sandstone formation with the appearance of a rose and the color of the red sand found in central Oklahoma.

NO MAN'S LAND

CHEROKEE.

Opened
Sept. 16, 1893

//////// 

UNASSIGNED LANDS
Opened by Land Run
April 22, 1889

CHEYENN
AND
ARAPAHO

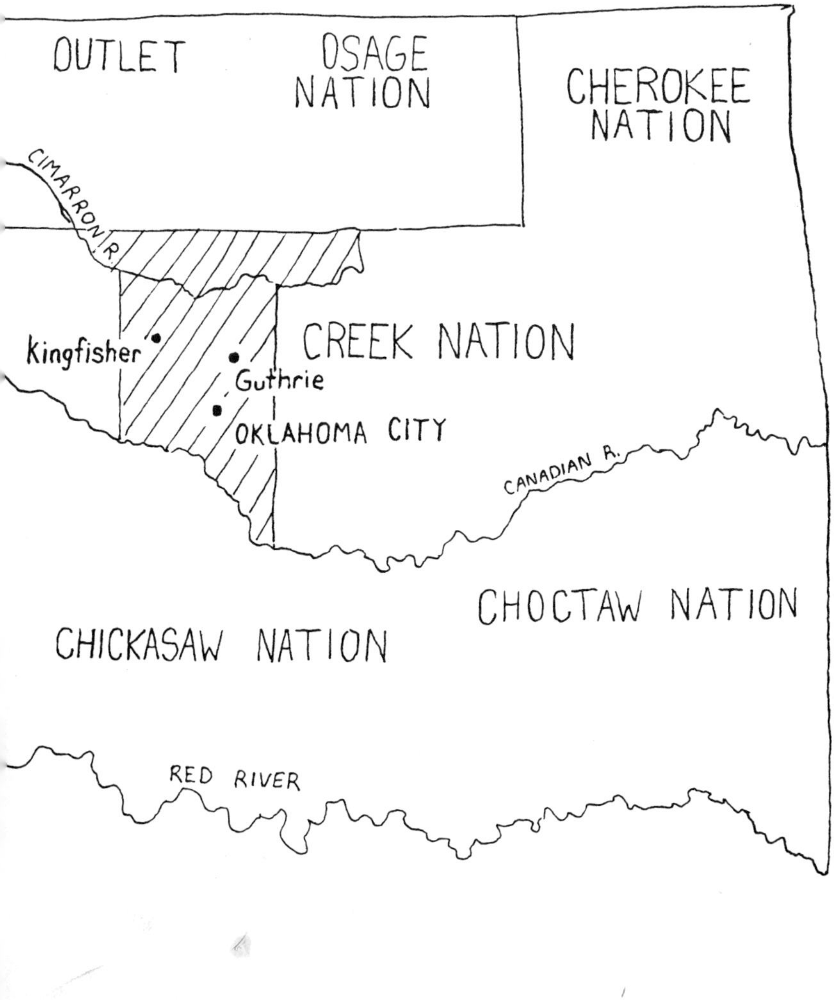
OUTLET
OSAGE NATION
CHEROKEE NATION
CIMARRON R.
Kingfisher
Guthrie
OKLAHOMA CITY
CREEK NATION
CANADIAN R.
CHOCTAW NATION
CHICKASAW NATION
RED RIVER

# About the Author

Carolyn Kirschstein and her husband reside in Broken Arrow, Oklahoma where she operates a pre-school for young children. After attending Oklahoma State and Oklahoma City Universities, she obtained a B.A. in biology with a minor in education. She has raised two children of her own and worked with the children of others for over twenty years.

Even though she has lived in several areas of the United States because of her father's career as a physician in the Air Force, she has roots in Oklahoma. These roots date back to the opening of the Cherokee Outlet in September, 1893, when two of her great-grandfathers claimed town lots in

Newkirk. One of them opened Newkirk's first bank. The other erected the first stone building in Newkirk. Her father can still relate stories of this opening as told to him personally by his grandfathers.

Both her parents were raised in Newkirk and after twenty-five years in the military returned to Guthrie to retire.

Ms. Kirschstein finds the history of Oklahoma interesting and unique and wants the children of the state to think so, too.

# About the Illustrator

David Merrell is a 16-year-old Guthrie High School student. He has studied art with Mary Beth Gilliland, Guthrie High School's art teacher. At the age of 7, he audited Drawing I and at the age of 13 audited Watercolor at Central State University in Edmond, Oklahoma. He has also studied with Western artist, Fred Olds.

Even though David was born in Bitburg, Germany on March 8, 1973 during his father's tour in the military, his roots in the town of Guthrie date back to the 1920's. His grandfather, who grew up in the Masonic Children's Home, later played football for Oklahoma University and graduated from OU's medical school.

After WWII, David's grandfather returned with his family to Guthrie where he set-up a general practice and served Guthrie as councilman and mayor during the 1950's.

David's father has also served as a leader in Guthrie's community affairs. During the restoration efforts in the early 1980's, David's father served as a councilman and as mayor of Guthrie.

In 1988 David entered a poster contest sponsored by The Farm Bureau entitled Art in Agriculture. David's was the winning poster for which he received $250. A limited edition of 1500 of the posters was printed. A picture of the poster appeared in the Farm Bureau's monthly newspaper.

Guthrie's Centennial Committee has
accepted David's entry as the official
centennial logo
for 1989.

It is David's plan to pursue a career in
commercial art.

# Why this book was written

As an educator, I became interested in providing a book to help the younger citizens of the state of Oklahoma understand the importance of the events of April 22, 1889. Many of our elementary schools schedule mock land runs every year during the week of the first historic land rush. The younger elementary children enjoy the events and participate in the festivities with enthusiasm, but many of them do not really understand what the celebrating is all about.

Even though the Taylor family is fictional, the events are historically accurate. Some of the events are a combination of what happened at more than one of the borders where the hungry land seekers gathered. I am aware that there was violence, dishonesty, and trickery before, during and after the run. This does not appear to be the place nor the age group to present these facts.

It is hoped that the story of Joey and Jane will provide teachers with a springboard for more discussion of the land rush and arouse questions about the run that could lead some of the older children to do further research on this period in Oklahoma history.

David's illustrations are wonderfully full of detail and I hope the children will enjoy and appreciate them. Notice the variety of people waiting to start the run, notice the squirrels in the trees by the Taylor family tent.

Look at the detail for yourself!

*Hooray for Oklahoma 1989*

*Carolyn Kirschstein*